Conscience

by VEDIKA AGARWAL

STORYMIRROR
Stories that reflect you

First Edition: May 2021

Typeset in Adobe Garamond Pro

ISBN: 978-81-951535-6-5

Cover Design: Prashant Gopal Gurav

Publisher: StoryMirror Infotech Pvt. Ltd.
                 145, First Floor, Powai Plaza, Hiranandani Gardens, Powai,
                 Mumbai - 400076, India

Web: https://storymirror.com
Facebook: https://facebook.com/storymirror
Twitter: https://twitter.com/story_mirror
Instagram: https://instagram.com/storymirror

Dedication

For my mother, father, maternal grandparents
and uncle Rahul Sharma

Acknowledgement

I would like to express my gratitude towards several people, but I've reduced the seemingly endless list to the most significant persons -

My mother who always stood up for my brother and I, sacrificing profusely to bring the plethora of happiness that home is. Without her constant support and encouragement, I don't think I could do even the most menial of things in life.

My father, who is invariably present to lift my spirits and enkindle bliss. I am often amused by the number of different ways he can make me feel proud of my work and appreciate the little things.

My maternal grandparents and uncle for being the guiding pillar, showering their blessings constantly and conveying the idea of making decisions subtly.

My kith and kin, who fueled my existence with their humor and read everything I wrote, despite the subject not being the one they adore. They joined in on my weirdness, listening to the most ludicrous of jokes. Many were the inspirations to the poems I wrote, and the most joyous times I ever had were the ones I spent with them.

Most importantly, I'd like to thank my professors since the beginning, who've instilled the seed of learning and growth in me. They provided the tools I needed to think outside the box, be industrious and work efficiently.

Preface

Writing, as cliche as it sounds, has always helped me escape reality and enter realms that sometimes go beyond human comprehension. When I write, there is this feeling of absolute control; where anything can be as quixotic as possible while I turn my imagination into words.

I spent much of my time concentrating on academics and sports until the novel coronavirus led to the two-month lockdown. For me, this was a blessing in disguise. In the beginning, I wrote poems revolving around my family members and relatives, oblivious to the fact that I have a flair for writing. Eventually I started introspecting on myself and writing about the most arbitrary things. For instance, the tree that stands muted in the summer air outside our house.

Speaking candidly, I hadn't the foggiest idea that the poems I'd written would be published. I just went along with the flow, writing when I was brimming with ideas.

Poetry made me truly appreciate a common saying: 'the pen is mightier than the sword'. Being able to express the swirling cloud of thoughts inside my mind with just words connected, making a shrine out of anything, and conveying simple messages in this evocative form has ignited my love for writing further.

Contents

1. Ripples of Sound

Trillions of sounds,
intricately combined.
Some as saccharine as chocolate,
some as esoteric as fate.

Innate lyrics in disparate genres,
remain forever.
When nothing is easy to express,
playing some will placate the stress.

Even alone,
it's a veracious friend.
As you twirl and groove,
your body in an unrestrained move.

It'll open your minds,
to doors of felicity.
As the words chime with your heart,
filling light in the dark.

When nobody stands,
it holds your hand.
Relating words you year to hear,
for endless years.

2. Word problems

More like a short narrative,
they are added to the paper.
Soon to become the most imperative -
while a few that distort the cerebrum.

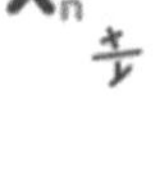

After much reading,
it finally makes sense.
And we start framing,
equations that are new-fangled enigmas.

Concepts are evaluated,
not with just one,
but myriads of long Hornets' nests.

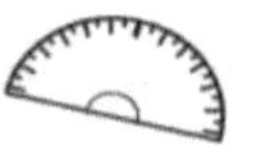

Even though the answer is known,
most remain obscure.
Only some clearly apprehend the unknown,
through methods of their own.

It couldn't have been any harder,
but they come up with many more.
Sometimes it takes an hour (oh dear!),
else a few minutes.

These conundrums come in unique dispositions,
to solve a few – a merriment,
and a few others – an everlasting punishment.

3. Witches' Wondery

Pointed hats,
coloured in contrasting shades.
Their harbingers black cats,
and their apprentice on crusades.

For many they exist.
For many, they're a notional
humanoid array.
Powerful forces they resist,
and the truth they won't say.

Castles engulfed in mist,
their shrill laughter resounding.
butchering in places on the list,
on brooms they come gyrating.

Spells and chants,
their way of learning.
Teleportation, flying and occult plants,
their esoteric realm of witching.

4. Time off

Amidst all the uproar,
we still find a place,
to untangle thyself of all furore,
and bask in the solace.

Taking divergent roads,
we reach our goal.
Be it the hills or the beach or
granny's abode,
and everything seems under
control.

No reason to scorn,
as we ride on the crest of waves.
Nothing to sweat our brows on –
and we discern the verisimilitude of all we crave.

An unwonted gaiety,
bliss on our physiognomy,
feelings of festivity.

Time seems to fly,
whilst we do everything we adore.
All workload consigned to oblivion – goodbye,
felicities come in galore.

5. Unbiological family

The sun is accompanied by the sky,
the wind accompanies those who fly.
And we are accompanied by friends,
who remain with us until the end.

Sharing rhapsodic moments with them,
spilling all the beams to them.
As invigorating as carbohydrates,
true friends are a part of everyone's fate.

It is unequivocally veracious,
that friends are solicitous.
They are the leaves of that sapling,
which grows with each moment of our living.

Friends look at you with a different vantage,
not letting you lose your mystique with age.
When your spirits need a lift,
friends are truly an extraordinary gift.

6. Tall story

Spreads like wildfire,
to some always dire.
Quite easy to say,
consequences hard to pay.

Yet they don't cease,
their numbers only increase.
When they say one,
they have to say another one.

Often to protect thyself,
concealing the truth about oneself.
Nobody realizes until they introspect,
that they'll soon lose all respect.

So many tales,
about this prevail.
Never lie,
or you'll never qualify.

7. Red Hue

It shines without glitter,
symbolizes nothing bitter.
The criterion of intimacy,
something many fancy.

Lies on the papery petals,
of roses that became instrumental.
When dusk drapes the sky,
sometimes the red magnifies.

Succumbs to the dark,
yet it leaves a mark.
Making the bright striking,
in its presence - outstanding.

The warmest of colours,
emanates a lot of power.
Many say it's negative,
but in my light, it's positive.

8. Revolving Blue

This orb of life,
in an aisle people jive.

Society's paradigm always changing,
the thread of sanity flickering.

Abundant facets make it off-centre,
from blue waters to talking figures.

Picturesque places in creation,
located in different nations.

Each year brings something new,
almost unsettling yet it's the golden hue.

Its celestial companions,
fascinate the mortal expansion.

Seen amidst the dark,
in green and blue it sparks.

Part of the universe,
protracting to fully traverse.

9. The Gaming orbit

Just within a few inches,
lie green and brown swathes of land,
on which men and women in stitches,
with armours and ammunition land.

Some sanctions the users,
to fabricate their own plot.
Some sanctions the users,
with warfare knowledge from the root.

Many fallacies revolve.
Some quite veracious,
some that fade after they evolve,
like the mist that's inauspicious.

Leading one into a world of wonder,
traveling in jeeps and tanks,
"Look for the red man up yonder!"
says the stalwart mate ready to attack.

We critters just live one life,
a shot on the heart taking us to the abyss.
But here, even if butchered by a knife -
there are two more lives that exist.

10. Reading realm

Turning the pages,
living in disparate ages.

From the youngest to the oldest,
sharing moments - from
happiest to saddest.

From this orb of pretence,
it takes you to one of
effervescence.

Sitting surrounded by four walls,
still, through foreign lands, you crawl.

On stands, they stand are placed,
in genre and languages, they're laced.

Fabricating tales that last forever,
connecting like family with the character.

11. Spirit of reverence

Dingy, despondent and dark –
despite the quagmire,
their smile will add a bright spark,
and their hug being the best pacifier.

Amongst all the sarcasm,
lies the essence of love.
With sheer enthusiasm,
they set a path for us to evolve.

They behave, speak and teach
like descendants from heaven.
A rectitude temperament they preach,
gaiety marking their presence.

Rever thy father and thy mother,
for without them –
this orb of life you won't discover,
and smarting will become hard to overcome.

12. Picking plaza

Motley of shops,
each in a unique colour-drop.
A gamut of products,
lining stands in fascinating conduct.

Hordes of people,
ages, height, colour - all unequal.
The subtle felicity of negotiations,
with owners at intermittent stations.

The theatres' display influencing,
what the man's physiognomy is presenting.
The scrumptious delicacies,
satisfying everyone's victual whimsies.

Almost out of the blue,
you meet known ones in the queue.
Then the clock starts ticking,
the catalyst of everyone hustling.

13. High descent

Inside might walls,
with gargantuan halls
and several members,
they live.

Often the rumours fly,
spreading a distance equal
to the sky.
Most of it remains a lie,
their sweet truth buried
by false notes.

Wars rage inside,
sometimes the unjust decide.
Armouries, ballrooms, and so much more.
Some let this fuel their ego.

Then comes the lineage,
giving rise to a new image.
Daughters held back,
sons in the grounds of hostility.

But there are souls,
magnanimity, and passion they hold.
They don't have to be a pretence,
it comes involuntarily from within.

14. Nine bolts

They crouched low,
as their shadows stretched ahead,
making the white line glow.

Adrenaline surged through them,
who sat unmoving,
on tracks spread a great extent.

Scrutinizing the athletes,
the referee brought up the gun,
as the shot's tumultuous noise peaked,

And they left their marks.
sprinting towards the end,
to their eyes, the rest is dark.

Pumping their arms,
pulling their body forward,
ensuring they break none of the norms,

Though one wins out of the rest,
just a second changing their rank,
they all gave their best.

15. Mortally immortal

She wakes up in the cold,
afraid it's past the time.
Burning the candle at both ends,
yet possessing this heart of gold.

Thinking of not just herself,
sacrificing profusely for the rest.
Her day extortionately hard,
unable to tranquilize thyself.

We celebrate days after her,
that comes once in a blue moon,
Shouldn't it be every day?
for regard she should receive is
beyond our measure.

The world a barren land,
without her sagacity and charms.
There would be no man,
for its imperative - her hand.

16. Outside the doors

Down winding roads,
experiencing the drop of the load.
Zephyrs peck our cheeks,
some straight, some oblique.

Crystalline waters rock back and forth,
as if purifying the yellow earth,
on which the golden medallion strikes,
lighting up the path for a hike.

The feeling's in a class by itself.
The charms of creation unwinding oneself.
Unfettered like the feathered friends,
we let our mundane bend.

Traveling from the hot to cold,
the comforts of abode on hold,
discerning what rests outside the doors.
It's never too late to explore.

17. Joie de vivre

Leading me into a world of effervescence,
making me agile.
It has become a part of my existence,
strengthening the fragile.

Parallel to laughter,
better than any placebo.
Fabricating an epoch brighter,
it has no incognito.

Imparting moments of equanimity,
cavorting and savouring -
Leading us out of reality,
and all come whilst playing.

I bask in these minutes of vividness,
that rise inside me.
The gaiety limitless,
rising over a great degree.

18. Inside blue waters

I always wonder:
how would it be underwater?
Apart from the green and the critters,
what else lies underwater?

Is there another realm?
adorned with blue spells and corals.
Habited by mermaids and nymph-like personnel,
as enticing as its iridescent floral.

What if this quixotic existed -
inside the blue waters?
Where the bliss clears the rusted -
remnants of our wrecked vehicles that deliver.

That lies uncharted,
on soft sea beds.
Not tarnished,
like the fine flower beds.

19. Half Apocalypse

Little did we know,
the morass that would come along,
as it began high up north,
the plague that would last long.

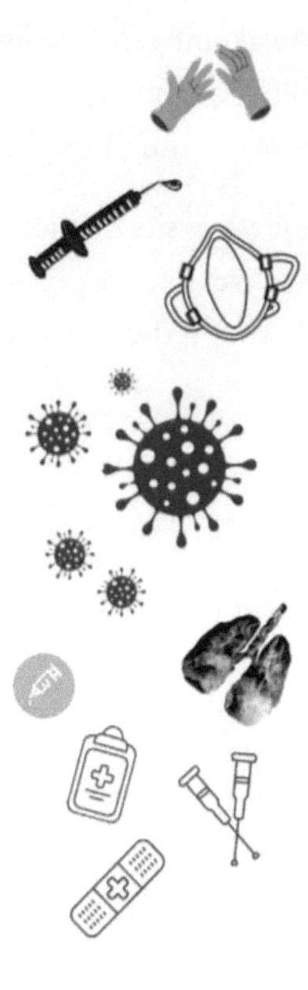

A month of Sundays, it seemed,
yet it bestowed lessons umpteen.
New-fangled activities imbued in our
existence,
and accentuation amplified on hygiene.

The affliction didn't cease,
although the prior fright did.
Many confronted the torment,
many remained in the cement-lids.
Whilst few unfettered souls roamed.

The needs had morphed,
one being the cruciality of electronics.
As the human race acculturated,
to the unprecedented pandemic.

Winds howled louder than before,
the natural forces sensing emancipation,
Not afraid of their own shadow any longer,
the critters traipsed in all locations.

Free rein,
quite ubiquitous it became, again.
Months had passed,
the economy a dried membrane.

20. First light

Awakening at first light -
blur for a while,
is everything in sight.

Dew - it sits outside,
On the papery green,
Marking the arrival of dawn.

Tiny zephyrs prance,
pleasantries on way,
another day, another chance.

With ease it appears,
as the blue bubbles move apart,
and the night's tenebrosity disappears.

Awakening at first light -
blur for a while,
is everything in sight.

21. Abuelos Maternos

Galore of stories,
their mystique eternal.
Riding through an ancient safari,
experiencing moments quite whimsical.

When am knocked sideways,
after a rebuke from the progenitors,
your golden words come like the sun's rays,
making joy stretch beyond the hemispheres.

You can enter my heart,
seeing your smile engraved inside.
With a wisecrack, you start,
a long conversation during many nights.

Brightening the mood with sweet songs -
and delicacies second to none.
Showing me what's right and wrong,
shining pearls amongst everyone.

22. Dead of night

In its depth, everything is hidden,
only the brightest not forbidden.
The shadows disappear,
and for some, it reigns - fear.

When the golden medallion goes down,
it wears its invisible crown.
Harbinger of golden sparks,
whose lustre - accentuates the dark.

Zephyrs dance across the town,
the nocturnal brush away the daytime frown.
The grid switches on the lights,
aiding commute for those in flight.

Some stay awake frolicking,
some lost in lands whilst sleeping.
In places, silence is rife,
in some the music ringing as they jive.

23. Essence of poetry

On parchments and more,
wherever they are stored.
Poems fly in the wind,
with invisible wings.

A fallacy it became -
they are just words that came.
But I see it in everything,
from the sand below to the sky above.

Though inanimate,
It is an eternal mate.
Some gallop for years within,
some travel for generations unknown.

Comes in forms umpteen,
portraying unforgettable scenes.
Transporting floating memories,
that perch perpetually in the soul.

24. Sparks in cactus

Where seeds can't grow,
it puts on the most ethereal of shows.
Drawing water in vertical extent,
then, it augments.

Oblivious to the fact:
that it keeps the critters intact.
Yet they say it's a thorny stick,
ready to pick.

Standing alone under the seething sun,
inside the spiny stem, the reaction has begun.
It stores the victual in cells,
using it when the cold fell.

Blossoms yet,
the foreigner it cuts and forgets.
It is beyond comparison,
the Euphorbia, its cousin.

25. Dear dad

From the depths of the sea,
through the icy waters,
you come up like that apple tree,
even taller.

The finest protector,
satisfying all my desires.
You stand in the centre,
my euphoria's amplifier.

Our bucket-list,
half similar,
with a gamut of twists.

I can talk about anything,
without the fear of being chastised.
You listen unmoving,
joining in energized.

From the depths of the sea,
through the icy waters,
you come up like that apple tree,
even taller.

I wouldn't want anyone,
because I know I have you -
the unsurpassable one.

26. Culinary round

On a rectangular stove,
thy can make fried bread like a dove.
Adding spices with measure,
to make dishes we treasure.

Cakes, pastries, pizzas, and pasta,
severed in magnificent plazas.
Hours we spend,
as the abodes of ingredients, we attend.

Fabricating recipes of our own,
pedantically chopping the outgrown.
The flames heat the motley of vivers,
Producing crisp grubs or a luscious river.

Taking only sufficient,
not wasting to be efficient.
the creation parallels to the elixir of life,
and in plates, it arrives.

27. Corollary of laughter

Comes like the stars at night,
a galore of thyself it brings.
Placates the tension and sparks ignite,
in any place, at any time.

Even strangers unite,
in its unfathomable presence.
It sets everything right,
but sometimes a misconception.

A pleasant sound,
as contagious as a plague.
It spreads around,
and only subsides after long.

Laughter, we call it,
that makes our stomachs ache.
Throughout the place it transmits,
how indispensable it is!

A medicine par excellence,
an exercise that's never exhausting.
Even a pretence,
seems side-splitting, usually.

28. Bucketing down

It hits hard on the window,
as the transparent lines head down.

Morphs the air to cold,
with drops, the clouds no longer hold.

Quagmires - it gives birth to,
its effects take a day or many to undo.

In some lands they say,
it comes after hours of pray.

Splattering like beats,
waning the heat.

A drink to the autotrophs,
but a hindrance to the heterotrophs.

Yet it stands crucial,
its absence - a spell too brutal.

It spreads those pygmy critters,
afflicting us with an ailment very bitter.

Despite its dark side,
it falls with pride.

29. Four Quarters

Spread across the court,
passing the ball amongst them in
cavort,
were just ten members,
unwilling to surrender.

Few went for a fast break,
each shot came with a loud creak.
Putting in action their scheme,
their adroitness in sheer gleam.

One took stance,
reaching out for the ball in
advance.
Whilst the other blocked the rival,
awaiting the guards' arrival.

As the ball went through the
basket,
the swish classic,
with no impediment in its path,
the opponent doing the score's math.

Victory not the only goal,
synergy, speed, and control.
Their eyes making observations astute,
moving in transfixing routes.

30. Land of Nod

The stars rose higher,
that were concealed,
during the stretch of the day,
unable to wait any longer.

All of it seems unbelievable,
be it something fortunate or malicious.
Yet you escape the reality,
experiencing that sphere in a state stable.

You see phantoms,
or charismatic sights.
And it can't be guaranteed,
if you remember even some.

You watch the mortal rim break,
the mind unfettered.
These golden bubbles traverse,
and the candid psyche is awake.

Nothing has to make sense,
in this domain of yours.
You find a spark within,
that's the essence.

Dreams,
with their wavering forms,
produce incredulous gasps,
and images supreme.